YO-DNL-779

The Very Patient Pony

by Susan Taylor Brown

illustrations by Linda Sniffen

published by **WRITERS PRESS**

For Barbara Regier, Debbie Regier,
and Barbara Mara at the Lazy R Ranch,
with loving thanks for all your heartfelt work
with Patient Ponies for Special People.
Over the years, the three of you have made
many children smile
and taught us all about
the healing powers of horses.

Susan Taylor Brown

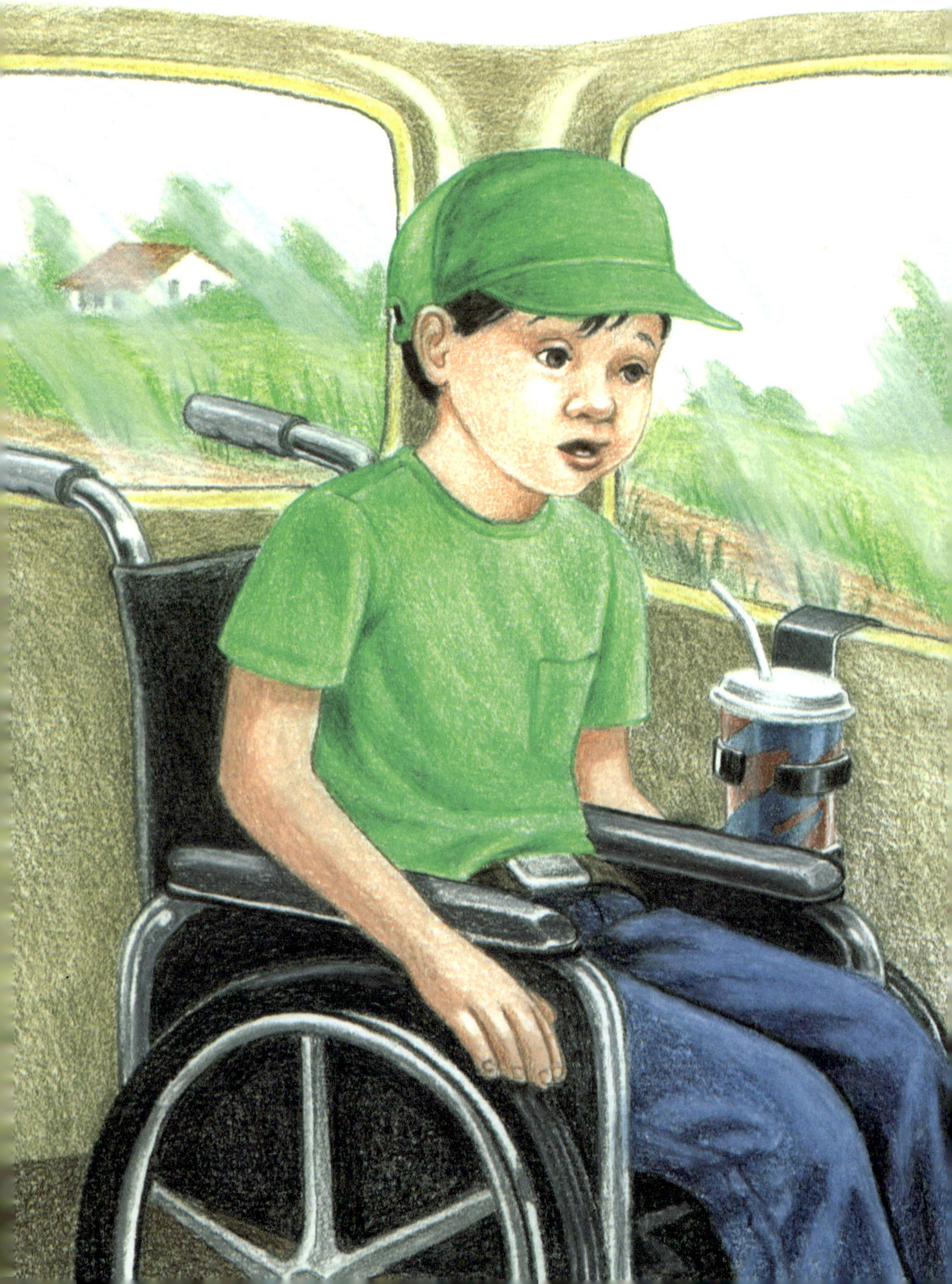

"Horses smell funny," said Eric. He rolled his hands across the top of his wheelchair.

"Why can't I go swimming? Why do I have to learn to ride a horse?"

"It will be fun," said Mother. "You will make new friends. Some of them will go to your new school."

"There's nothing wrong with my old friends," said Eric. He stared out the window in the back of the van. It was too late. They were already at camp.

Eric met Debbie, the camp leader. He saw lots of kids on horses. No one else had a wheelchair. Eric needs a wheelchair because a car accident left him disabled.

"My stomach hurts," said Eric. "I want to go home."

"Are you sick?" asked Mother.

Eric shook his head.

"Are you scared?"

"No," said Eric. But inside he was very scared. He didn't want to ride a horse. Not ever. Never!

Eric sat in his wheelchair and watched. Five kids rode horses. Four of them went slow. A girl on a black pony went fast.

They ran past Eric. They ran around a barrel. Then they ran back to the fence and stopped.

"Hi," she said, "my name is Heather."

"Hi." said Eric.

"This is Midnight," she said. "He's blind. Do you want to ride him?"

"No," said Eric. "My stomach hurts. I better not ride right now."

"Are you sick?" asked Heather.

"No, my stomach just hurts."

"You're scared."

"I am not." said Eric. But inside he was scared. He didn't want to ride a horse. Not ever. Never!

Eric watched Debbie feed the horses. They all ran in to eat.

One pony could not get any hay. A big horse chased him away.

"Debbie," he said. "That pony is hungry."

"That's okay," said Debbie. "Joe is a patient pony."

"What does patient mean?"

"It means Joe will eat later. He will wait until the time is right."

"Why can't Joe eat now?"

"Because he is scared. He is afraid of Annie, the big horse."

"It's not fair," said Eric. "Joe should eat when he is hungry."

"It's not fair you need a wheelchair," said Debbie.

"Are you ready to go for a ride today?" asked Debbie.

He shook his head. He waited for Debbie to ask if he was scared. Debbie just smiled.

Eric rolled his wheelchair close to the fence. He wished he had a carrot to give Joe. Maybe then Joe would come close and Eric could scratch his ears.

"I will wait with you," Eric told Joe. "Maybe then you won't be scared."

Then it happened again. Debbie threw out the hay. Joe ran in. Annie chased him away.

Eric looked out in the pasture. The horses ran around. They all looked like friends, even Annie and Joe.

Debbie brought Joe out of the pasture so he could eat some oats.

"Would you like Joe to stand by you?" she asked.

"No." said Eric.

Joe didn't look so little anymore. He wondered what it would be like to ride Joe. He wondered if Joe was as fast as Midnight. Then he got a funny upside down feeling in his stomach. He stopped wondering.

Eric watched the other kids ride Joe. Some kids wanted to go fast. But Joe liked to go slow. Eric laughed.

"Would you like to ride today?" asked Debbie.

"No." said Eric. "But maybe I could brush Joe a little bit?"

Debbie brought him a brush. Joe nibbled grass. Eric ran the brush over his side. He put his hand against Joe's coat. It felt soft and warm.

Heather brought Midnight over to stand near Joe.

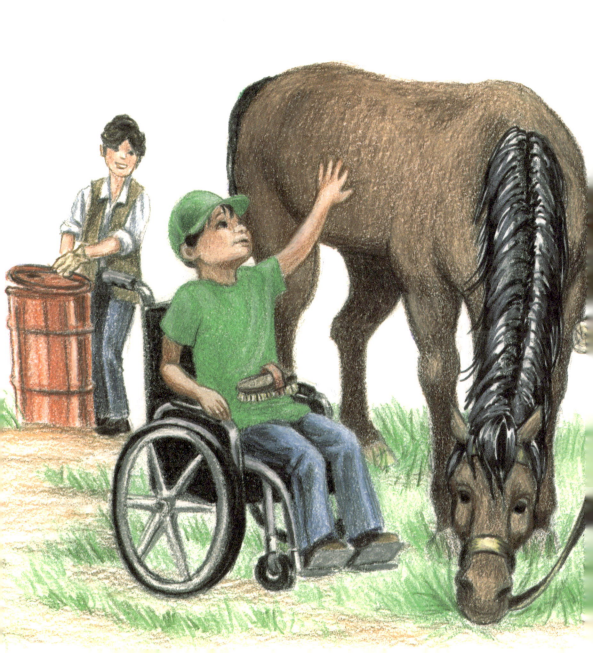

"I have a secret." said Heather.

"What?" asked Eric.

"When I came to camp, I didn't want to ride Midnight. I thought he would hurt me. The first time I rode him I was scared."

"I bet Midnight got scared when he couldn't see anymore," said Eric.

Heather nodded. "Now I know Midnight won't hurt me. We are a good team." She scratched Midnight between the ears. "You and Joe could be a team too. Then Joe can take you places you can't go with your wheelchair."

Joe moved closer to Eric. He pushed his nose around Eric's shirt, looking for a piece of apple.

Eric thought about it all day. He didn't want to leave his wheelchair, but he wanted to sit on Joe's back.

He was scared but he had been patient. Now he was ready.

"The time is right," Eric told Debbie. "I want to ride."

Debbie helped him up on Joe's back. The saddle felt different from his wheelchair. She showed him how to use the reins to make Joe turn. She showed him how to pull on the reins to make Joe stop. Since he couldn't kick with his feet, she showed him how to make a clicking noise with his tongue to make Joe walk.

"Are you ready?" asked Debbie.

Eric saw Heather sitting on Midnight. She smiled at him.

"I'm ready." said Eric.

"Tell Joe you are ready to go." said Debbie.

Eric made the clicking sound with his tongue. Joe turned his head to look at him. Then he started forward.

Eric pulled back on the reins and Joe stopped. Eric made the clicking noise again. Joe took a few more steps. When Debbie knew he was safe, she took off the lead rope. Eric made Joe walk in a big circle.

He smiled at Debbie and Heather. "This is fun." he said.

"I know you could do it." said Debbie.

Eric just kept smiling. He didn't want to stop riding. Not now, not ever!

More great children's books that include ALL children!

—— Enrichment Collection Set #2 ——

Becca & Sue Make Two by Sandra Haines
With practice and cooperation, *together we're better.*

Donnie Makes A Difference by Sandra Haines
Perseverance wins in this inspirational story.

My Friend Emily by Susanne Swanson
Helping through friendship and understanding.

Lee's Tough Time Rhyme by Susanne Swanson
Preparation conquers challenges.

The Boy on the Bus by Diana Loski
Understanding teaches lessons in friendship.

Dinosaur Hill by Diana Loski
Adventure without limitations.

Zack Attacks by Diana Loski
Success in spite of adversity.

—— Other inclusion-minded books ——

Eagle Feather
by Sonia Gardner, illustrated by James Spurlock
A *special edition* treasure of Native American values in stunning artwork.

Catch a Poetic Hodgepodge
by Kevin Boos, illustrated by Paul Hart
A whimsical collection of poems especially written for children.

1-800-574-1715
www.writerspress.com

WRITERS PRESS
5278 CHINDEN BLVD.
GARDEN CITY, ID 83714